CareBears™

Caring Contest

by Nancy Parent
Illustrated by David Stein

SCHOLASTIC INC.
New York   Toronto   London
Auckland   Sydney   Mexico City
New Delhi   Hong Kong   Buenos Aires

ISBN 0-439-45158-2

12 11 10 9 8 7 6 5 4 3 2 1

2 3 4 5 6 7/0

Printed in the U.S.A.
First Scholastic printing, August 2002

One day, Cheer Bear decided to hold a Care-a-lot caring contest. "A prize will go to the bear who shows the best way to care," she said.

First Annual Care-a-lot Caring Contest

The Care Bears took the contest very seriously. Friend Bear was the first to see a way to care. "I think caring means taking turns with a favorite toy," she said.

Share Bear cared by making sure she had enough treats for everyone. "Help yourself!" she said as she passed out yummy rainbow bars.

When Wish Bear wanted a push on her swing,
Good Luck Bear was there.
"Lucky you stopped by!" said Wish Bear.
"Caring is helping when you're needed,"
Good Luck Bear replied.

During an afternoon storm, Grumpy Bear saw a
way to care for Friend Bear. "Caring," said Grumpy
Bear, "is sharing your umbrella in the rain."

When Share Bear didn't feel well, some of her friends visited her. "Comforting someone who is sick shows you really care," Tenderheart Bear said.

"Caring is making someone laugh when he's sad," said Funshine Bear. He juggled stars to cheer up Grumpy Bear.

"I can show I care by letting you go ahead of me in line," Wish Bear told Love-a-lot Bear. "I'd love to!" said Love-a-lot Bear. "Thanks!"

When Wish Bear couldn't fall asleep at naptime, Bedtime Bear read her a sweet dreams story to show he cared.

Love-a-lot Bear showed how to care by giving Tenderheart Bear a great big hug. "I love you, Tenderheart Bear," she said.

Cheer Bear thought all the Care Bears had done a wonderful job of caring. But who should she pick as the winner of the contest?

Cheer Bear made her announcement: "The winners of the Care-a-lot caring contest are . . . all of you! Because everyone wins when everyone cares for others!" Then she proudly handed out the prizes.

"Now we can show how much we care by sharing these prizes with our friends!" all the Care Bears said together. And that's just what they did.

Three cheers for caring, Care Bears!